Every weekend my Grandpa
went fishing,

He said he had friends in the
sea he was meeting.

Grandma just laughed and packed us a bag,

As today I was going, and I was so glad

I patiently watched the gentle, bright sea,

"To see a whale today, what a
    surprise that would be."

Grandpa chuckled, "just keep watch over there!"
He yawned, falling asleep, taking in the fresh air.

I sat and I waited to see a whale in
the view,

For I had loved them forever and
Grandpa had too!

I almost gave up, when the sea
bubbled and grew,

And a friendly low voice came bellowing
through.

"I can't believe my eyes" smiled
the big whale, Blue.

"Your Grandpa's my friend, he's
told me lots about you!"

Handing me his fins we had a
big, soggy cuddle,

I looked like I'd been jumping in lots of
wet puddles!

Grandpa awoke, "Oh Blue, you are here,"

"I've caught you a snack" he grinned
ear to ear.

We talked and we laughed at the stories they
shared,
They had a great friendship, nothing else
could compare!

"A whale as a friend, wow, what a surprise,"
"But I don't know how I will leave all this behind!"

"My angel you won't, we'll be back every week,
or a friendship with a whale is a one we must keep!"

As it turned dark, Blue started to
yawn,

So we said our goodbyes and
headed back home.

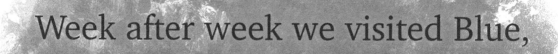

Week after week we visited Blue,

Until weeks turned to years and our
friendships but grew.

Colour me in!

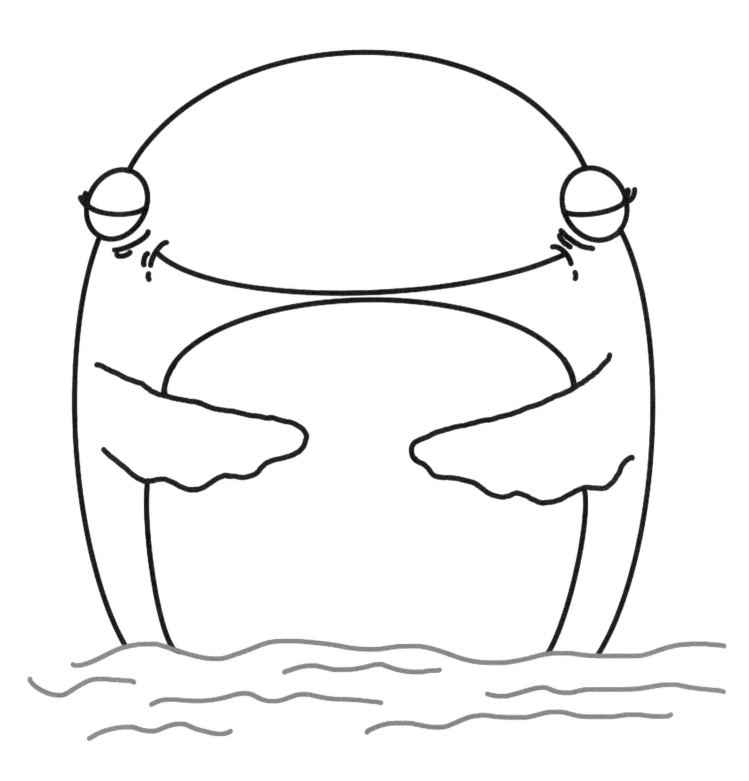

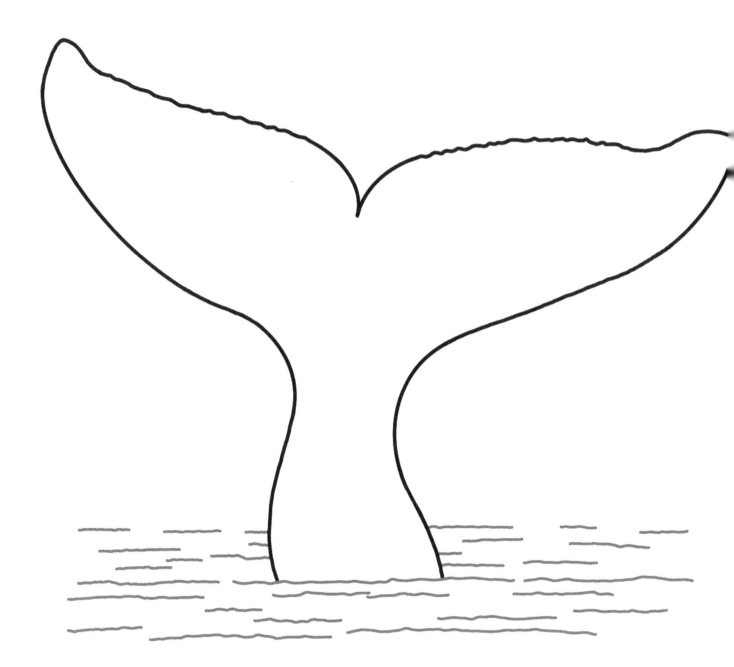

Spot the difference
(6 differences)

Connect the dots!

Lightning Source UK Ltd.
Milton Keynes UK
UKHW050905060721
386704UK00006B/47